Awakening the Passion

Nova T. Rae

Published by Palette of Intrigue, 2024.

AWAKENING THE PASSION

First edition. June 26, 2024.

ISBN: 979-8224538942

Written by Nova T. Rae.

Chapter 1: Awakening the Passion

The sun dipped below the horizon, casting a golden hue over the mystical land of Elysia. Elara stood at the edge of the ancient library, her fingers tracing the intricate carvings on the wooden door. Her heart raced with anticipation. She had heard whispers of a hidden chamber, a place where the most powerful and forbidden tomes were kept.

Taking a deep breath, she pushed the door open and stepped inside. The library was a labyrinth of towering shelves, each filled with books that held the secrets of the ages. As she wandered through the aisles, she felt a strange pull guiding her deeper into the maze of knowledge.

Her steps led her to a secluded corner where a hidden door was cleverly concealed behind a tapestry depicting a scene of celestial beings. Elara's fingers trembled as she moved the tapestry aside and revealed the door. She whispered a few words of magic, and the door creaked open, revealing a dimly lit chamber.

Inside, the air was thick with the scent of aged parchment and ancient spells. Shelves lined the walls, filled with books bound in leather and adorned with arcane symbols. In the center of the room, a single book lay on a pedestal, bathed in a soft, ethereal glow.

Elara approached the pedestal, her eyes wide with wonder. The book seemed to call to her, its energy pulsating through the air. She reached out and touched the cover, feeling a surge of warmth travel up her arm. With a deep breath, she opened the book and began to read.

As she turned the pages, Elara felt a strange heat building within her. The words seemed to weave a spell around her, awakening sensations she had never experienced before. Her breath quickened, and her cheeks flushed with a mix of excitement and curiosity. The book spoke of sensual magic, a forbidden art that intertwined desire and power.

Lost in the pages, Elara didn't notice the figure approaching her until a hand gently touched her shoulder. She gasped and turned to see Kael, her mentor, standing behind her. His eyes, dark and intense, bore into hers with a mixture of concern and intrigue.

"What are you doing here, Elara?" Kael's voice was soft, yet it held an edge of authority.

"I...I found this book," Elara stammered, her heart pounding in her chest. "I couldn't resist."

Kael's gaze shifted to the book, and his expression hardened. "This is dangerous magic, Elara. It is not something to be taken lightly."

"I know," she replied, her voice barely a whisper. "But I felt...drawn to it."

Kael sighed and closed the book, his fingers brushing against hers. The touch sent a shiver down Elara's spine, and she found herself longing for more. She could see the struggle in Kael's eyes, the battle between duty and desire.

"You must be careful," Kael said, his voice tinged with a hint of something deeper. "These powers can consume you if you're not prepared."

Elara nodded, but her mind was still reeling from the sensations the book had awakened. As Kael turned to leave, she reached out and grabbed his hand, stopping him in his tracks.

"Kael, wait," she pleaded. "Teach me. Help me understand this magic."

Kael looked at her, his expression unreadable. For a moment, the world seemed to stand still. Then, with a resigned sigh, he nodded. "Very well, Elara. But know this: once you start down this path, there is no turning back."

Elara's heart leaped with a mixture of fear and excitement. She had always admired Kael, his strength, his wisdom, and his enigmatic charm. Now, she would have the chance to learn from him in ways she had never imagined.

Over the following days, their training sessions took on a new intensity. Kael taught her to channel her desires, to harness the sensual energy that flowed through her. Their interactions became charged with a tension that was both exhilarating and terrifying.

One evening, as they practiced in the secluded grove behind the library, the air was thick with the scent of blooming flowers and the soft hum of magic. Kael stood behind Elara, his hands guiding hers as they traced intricate symbols in the air.

"Feel the energy," Kael murmured, his breath warm against her ear. "Let it flow through you."

Elara closed her eyes and focused on the sensations coursing through her body. She could feel Kael's presence, strong and steady, grounding her as she navigated the currents of power. His hands moved to her shoulders, and she leaned back against him, feeling the warmth of his body.

"Good," Kael whispered, his voice sending a shiver down her spine. "You're doing well."

As they continued, Elara felt a growing heat within her, a fire that seemed to ignite every nerve in her body. She could feel Kael's breath quicken, matching her own. The air around them crackled with energy, and she knew that they were on the brink of something profound.

Without thinking, Elara turned in Kael's arms, her eyes locking onto his. For a moment, they simply stared at each other, the air between them heavy with unspoken desire. Then, as if drawn by an irresistible force, their lips met in a kiss that was both tender and fierce.

The world seemed to blur around them as they explored each other with a newfound urgency. Kael's hands roamed over Elara's body, awakening sensations she had never known. She clung to him, her fingers digging into his back as the fire within her burned brighter.

They pulled back, breathless, their foreheads resting together. "Elara," Kael whispered, his voice hoarse with emotion. "We must be careful."

"I know," she replied, her voice equally strained. "But I can't stop."

"Neither can I," Kael admitted, his eyes dark with desire. "But we must find a way to control this, to use it wisely."

Elara nodded, her mind spinning with the possibilities. She knew that their journey would be fraught with challenges, but she was ready to face them, as long as Kael was by her side.

As they stood together in the twilight, the grove around them seemed to pulse with the magic of their bond. Elara knew that this was just the beginning, and that their path would lead them to places they could never have imagined. But she was ready, and with Kael's guidance, she knew that she could master the sensual magic that flowed through her veins.

Their journey had just begun, and Elara felt a thrill of anticipation as she looked up at Kael, her mentor, her partner, and perhaps, one day, something more. Together, they would explore the depths of their desires and unlock the true potential of their powers, forging a bond that would transcend time and magic.

Chapter 2: The Forbidden Book

The days that followed their kiss were a whirlwind of emotion and discovery. Elara found herself constantly thinking about Kael, the way his touch had ignited something deep within her. She knew they were treading dangerous ground, but the pull was too strong to resist.

Each evening, they met in the hidden chamber, diving deeper into the sensual magic. Elara's understanding grew, but so did her longing for Kael. She could see the same desire reflected in his eyes, though he tried to maintain his composure.

One night, after an especially intense session, Kael closed the forbidden book and looked at Elara with a mix of frustration and yearning. "Elara, we need to talk."

She nodded, feeling her heart pound in her chest. "Yes, Kael?"

"This path we're on... it's dangerous," he began, his voice strained. "The magic we're dealing with isn't just about power. It's about desire, temptation. It can consume us if we're not careful."

"I understand," Elara replied, her eyes fixed on his. "But I don't want to stop."

Kael sighed, running a hand through his hair. "Neither do I. But we must find a balance. We need to control it, not let it control us."

Elara stepped closer, her heart aching with the need to touch him. "Teach me, Kael. Help me control it."

Their eyes locked, and for a moment, it felt as if the world had stopped. Then, with a resigned sigh, Kael nodded. "Very well. But we must be vigilant."

The next day, their training took on a new intensity. Kael pushed Elara harder, challenging her to harness her emotions without losing control. The exercises were grueling, but Elara welcomed the challenge. She could feel her power growing, her connection to Kael deepening.

One evening, as they practiced in the grove, Kael stood behind Elara, guiding her hands as they traced symbols in the air. The sun had set, and the only light came from the glowing runes they created.

"Feel the energy," Kael murmured, his breath warm against her ear. "Let it flow through you, but don't let it overwhelm you."

Elara closed her eyes and focused on the sensations coursing through her body. She could feel Kael's presence, strong and steady, grounding her as she navigated the currents of power. His hands moved to her shoulders, and she leaned back against him, feeling the warmth of his body.

"Good," Kael whispered, his voice sending a shiver down her spine. "You're doing well."

As they continued, Elara felt a growing heat within her, a fire that seemed to ignite every nerve in her body. She could feel Kael's breath quicken, matching her own. The air around them crackled with energy, and she knew that they were on the brink of something profound.

Without thinking, Elara turned in Kael's arms, her eyes locking onto his. For a moment, they simply stared at each other, the air between them heavy with unspoken desire. Then, as if drawn by an irresistible force, their lips met in a kiss that was both tender and fierce.

The world seemed to blur around them as they explored each other with a newfound urgency. Kael's hands roamed over Elara's body, awakening sensations she had never known. She clung to him, her fingers digging into his back as the fire within her burned brighter.

They pulled back, breathless, their foreheads resting together. "Elara," Kael whispered, his voice hoarse with emotion. "We must be careful."

"I know," she replied, her voice equally strained. "But I can't stop."

"Neither can I," Kael admitted, his eyes dark with desire. "But we must find a way to control this, to use it wisely."

Elara nodded, her mind spinning with the possibilities. She knew that their journey would be fraught with challenges, but she was ready to face them, as long as Kael was by her side.

As they stood together in the twilight, the grove around them seemed to pulse with the magic of their bond. Elara knew that this was just the beginning, and that their path would lead them to places they could never have imagined. But she was ready, and with Kael's guidance, she knew that she could master the sensual magic that flowed through her veins.

The following weeks were a blur of intense training and stolen moments of intimacy. Elara found herself growing more confident in her abilities, her control over the sensual magic becoming stronger. Kael was a patient and demanding teacher, pushing her to her limits while also offering the comfort and support she needed.

One evening, as they practiced in the hidden chamber, Kael handed Elara a new book. Its cover was adorned with intricate runes, and it seemed to pulse with a soft, inviting glow.

"This is the next step," Kael explained. "It's a more advanced text on sensual magic. It will help you deepen your understanding and control."

Elara took the book, feeling its warmth seep into her hands. "Thank you, Kael. I promise I won't let you down."

"I know you won't," he replied, his eyes softening as they met hers. "But remember, this magic is not just about power. It's about connection, trust, and balance."

As Elara delved into the new book, she found herself drawn deeper into the world of sensual magic. The spells and rituals were more complex, requiring a greater degree of focus and control. But with Kael's guidance, she began to master them, feeling her power grow with each passing day.

Their training sessions became more intense, the air between them charged with a palpable energy. Elara could feel the bond between them strengthening, their connection growing deeper and more profound. She knew that their journey was just beginning, and that there were many challenges ahead. But with Kael by her side, she felt ready to face whatever came their way.

One night, as they practiced in the grove, Kael suddenly pulled back, his expression troubled. "Elara, there's something I need to tell you."

She looked at him, her heart skipping a beat. "What is it, Kael?"

He took a deep breath, his eyes dark with emotion. "There's a reason why this magic is forbidden. It's not just because it's powerful. It's because it has the potential to consume us, to drive us to the brink of madness."

Elara's heart raced as she listened to Kael's words. "But we can control it, can't we? We can use it wisely."

Kael nodded, but his expression remained serious. "Yes, we can. But we must always be vigilant. We must never let our guard down, never let our desires overwhelm us."

Elara reached out and took Kael's hand, feeling the warmth of his skin against hers. "I trust you, Kael. And I trust myself. We can do this, together."

Kael's eyes softened as he looked at her, his expression filled with a mixture of love and determination. "Yes, we can. Together."

As they stood there, the night air filled with the scent of blooming flowers and the soft hum of magic, Elara felt a deep sense of peace. She knew that their journey would be challenging, but she also knew that they were stronger together. With Kael by her side, she felt ready to face whatever came their way, confident in their bond and the power of their love.

Their journey had just begun, and Elara felt a thrill of anticipation as she looked up at Kael, her mentor, her partner, and perhaps, one day, something more. Together, they would explore the depths of their desires and unlock the true potential of their powers, forging a bond that would transcend time and magic.

Chapter 3: Desire Unleashed

The air was thick with anticipation as Elara and Kael entered the hidden chamber once more. Each step they took together seemed to deepen the unspoken bond between them. The room was filled with the soft glow of magical runes, casting dancing shadows on the walls. The energy in the air crackled with a mix of power and desire.

Kael led Elara to the center of the room, where an intricate circle of symbols was drawn on the floor. "Today, we will explore the next level of our training," he said, his voice steady but tinged with an underlying excitement. "You must learn to harness your desires and transform them into pure magical energy."

Elara nodded, her heart pounding in her chest. She could feel the intensity of Kael's gaze, the warmth of his presence enveloping her. As she stepped into the circle, she felt a surge of power course through her veins, heightening her senses.

Kael moved to stand behind her, his hands hovering just above her shoulders. "Close your eyes," he instructed, his breath warm against her ear. "Feel the energy within you, the desires that fuel your magic. Let them flow through you, but do not let them control you."

Elara closed her eyes and focused on the sensations coursing through her body. She could feel the heat building within her, a fire that seemed to ignite every nerve. Her breath quickened, and she leaned back slightly, feeling the comforting presence of Kael just behind her.

"Good," Kael murmured, his voice a soothing balm to her heightened senses. "Now, channel that energy. Let it flow through your body and into the symbols around you."

Elara concentrated, visualizing the energy within her transforming into streams of light that flowed from her fingertips. She felt the runes beneath her feet respond, glowing brighter as they absorbed the magic. The air around them hummed with power, and Elara could feel the connection between herself and Kael growing stronger.

As the energy continued to flow, Kael's hands gently touched her shoulders, guiding her movements. The touch was electric, sending a shiver down her spine. She could feel his breath against her neck, warm and inviting, and it took all her focus to maintain control.

"You're doing well," Kael whispered, his voice filled with pride. "But remember, control is key. Do not let your desires overwhelm you."

Elara nodded, taking a deep breath to steady herself. She could feel the intensity of their connection, the unspoken desires that simmered beneath the surface. It was both exhilarating and terrifying, but she knew she had to master it.

With each passing moment, the energy within the room grew stronger. The runes pulsed with light, reflecting the power that flowed through Elara and Kael. She could feel the magic weaving around them, creating a bond that was both powerful and intimate.

Suddenly, the air around them seemed to shift, and Elara felt a wave of warmth wash over her. She opened her eyes to find Kael standing in front of her, his gaze locked onto hers. The intensity in his eyes took her breath away, and she could feel her own desires mirrored in his.

Without a word, Kael reached out and took her hand, his touch sending a jolt of electricity through her body. He pulled her closer, their bodies almost touching. The air between them was charged with unspoken longing, and Elara could feel her heart racing.

"Elara," Kael whispered, his voice filled with a mix of emotion and desire. "This path we are on... it requires trust, and a deep connection. Are you ready for that?"

Elara met his gaze, her eyes filled with determination. "Yes, Kael. I'm ready."

A small smile tugged at the corners of Kael's lips, and he squeezed her hand gently. "Good. Because from this moment on, we are bound by more than just our magic. We are bound by our desires, our trust, and our commitment to each other."

Elara felt a surge of emotion at his words, a sense of unity and purpose that filled her with strength. She knew that their journey would not be easy, but she also knew that they were stronger together.

As they stood there, hand in hand, the runes around them pulsed with a radiant light. The magic within the chamber seemed to respond to their bond, weaving around them in a protective embrace. Elara could feel the energy flowing through her, a powerful force that was fueled by their connection.

Kael's eyes softened as he looked at her, his expression filled with a deep, unspoken affection. "Elara," he murmured, his voice barely above a whisper. "You are more powerful than you realize. Together, we can achieve great things."

Elara felt a warmth spread through her at his words, a sense of pride and determination. She knew that their journey was just beginning, and that there would be many challenges ahead. But with Kael by her side, she felt ready to face whatever came their way.

As the night deepened, they continued their training, exploring the depths of their magic and their connection. Each moment brought them closer, their bond growing stronger with every touch, every shared breath.

By the time the first light of dawn began to filter through the windows, Elara felt a deep sense of accomplishment. She had harnessed her desires, transformed them into pure magical energy, and forged a bond with Kael that transcended the physical.

As they stood together, bathed in the soft glow of the rising sun, Elara knew that they were on the brink of something extraordinary. Their journey was just beginning, and the path ahead was filled with possibilities.

With Kael by her side, she felt ready to explore the depths of her power, to face whatever challenges lay ahead. Together, they would unlock the true potential of their magic, and forge a bond that would withstand the test of time.

Their journey had just begun, and Elara felt a thrill of anticipation as she looked up at Kael, her mentor, her partner, and perhaps, one day, something more. Together, they would explore the depths of their desires and unlock the true potential of their powers, forging a bond that would transcend time and magic.

Chapter 4: The Enchanted Forest

The morning sun bathed the land of Elysia in a warm, golden light as Elara and Kael prepared for their journey. Today, they were venturing into the Enchanted Forest, a mystical place known for its rare magical ingredients and ancient secrets. Elara felt a mix of excitement and trepidation. The forest was beautiful but unpredictable, filled with creatures and plants that could both enchant and endanger.

Kael handed Elara a small, leather-bound journal. "This will help you identify the ingredients we need," he explained. "The forest is a living entity, and it responds to our intentions. Stay close to me, and be mindful of your surroundings."

Elara nodded, her heart pounding with anticipation. She could feel the magical energy of the forest even before they entered it, a soft hum that vibrated through the air. As they stepped past the tree line, the world around them seemed to change. The light became softer, filtered through the dense canopy of leaves above, casting dappled shadows on the forest floor.

They walked in silence, the only sounds the rustling of leaves and the occasional call of a distant bird. The air was thick with the scent of earth and blooming flowers, a heady mixture that heightened Elara's senses. She could feel the magic in the air, a living, breathing presence that seemed to watch their every move.

Kael led the way, his movements confident and sure. Elara followed closely, her eyes wide with wonder. Everywhere she looked, she saw signs of the forest's enchantment—flowers that glowed with an inner light, trees that seemed to whisper secrets, and streams that sparkled like liquid silver.

They soon reached a clearing, bathed in a soft, ethereal glow. In the center stood a massive tree, its branches stretching towards the sky like welcoming arms. At its base grew a cluster of flowers with petals that shimmered in a rainbow of colors.

"These are Lumina Blossoms," Kael explained, kneeling to examine the flowers. "They are essential for the spell we need. Their essence can amplify our magic."

Elara knelt beside him, carefully picking the blossoms and placing them in a small pouch. As she worked, she felt a sudden surge of energy, a warmth that spread through her body. She glanced up at Kael, who was watching her with a mixture of pride and something deeper, something that made her heart race.

"Good," Kael said softly, his eyes locking onto hers. "You're becoming more attuned to the magic around you."

Elara smiled, feeling a flush rise to her cheeks. "Thank you, Kael. I couldn't have done it without you."

They continued their journey, collecting various ingredients and encountering the forest's many wonders. As the day wore on, Elara felt her connection to Kael growing stronger, their bond deepening with each shared experience.

In the late afternoon, they reached a serene glade, its tranquility broken only by the gentle babble of a stream. Kael paused, his eyes scanning the area. "We'll rest here for a while," he said, setting down his pack.

Elara sat on the soft grass, feeling the cool breeze against her skin. The forest seemed to envelop them in a cocoon of peace, its magic a soothing presence. She closed her eyes and took a deep breath, savoring the moment.

Kael sat beside her, his presence a comforting anchor. "Elara," he said quietly, his voice tinged with emotion. "I need to tell you something."

Elara opened her eyes and turned to him, her heart pounding. "What is it, Kael?"

He hesitated, his gaze intense. "The bond we share... it's more than just teacher and student. The magic we wield, the connection we feel—it's unlike anything I've ever experienced."

Elara's breath caught in her throat. She could feel the truth of his words, the depth of their bond. "I feel it too, Kael," she whispered, her voice barely audible. "It's like we're connected on a level I can't explain."

Kael reached out and took her hand, his touch sending a jolt of electricity through her. "This journey we're on, it's not just about mastering magic. It's about understanding ourselves, our desires, and our connection to each other."

Elara's heart swelled with emotion. She could feel the magic of the forest weaving around them, amplifying their connection. "Kael," she said, her voice trembling. "I want to explore this bond with you, to understand it fully."

Kael's eyes softened, a small smile playing on his lips. "As do I, Elara. But we must be careful. The magic we share is powerful, and it can easily overwhelm us if we're not vigilant."

Elara nodded, her resolve strengthening. "I understand. We'll face it together, whatever comes our way."

Kael squeezed her hand, his gaze filled with a mixture of affection and determination. "Together," he agreed.

As the sun began to set, casting a warm, golden glow over the glade, Elara and Kael sat in companionable silence, their hands intertwined. The forest around them seemed to hum with approval, its magic a gentle, protective presence.

As darkness fell, they set up camp, a small fire crackling in the center of the glade. Elara felt a sense of contentment she had never known, a deep peace that came from being with Kael, from knowing that they were on this journey together.

Later that night, as they lay beneath the stars, Elara felt a warmth spread through her. She turned to Kael, her heart full. "Kael," she said softly, "thank you for everything."

Kael looked at her, his eyes reflecting the starlight. "Thank you, Elara, for trusting me, for sharing this journey with me."

Elara reached out and touched his face, feeling the warmth of his skin beneath her fingertips. "We're in this together," she whispered. "No matter what."

Kael leaned in, his lips brushing against hers in a gentle, tender kiss. The world around them seemed to fade away, leaving only the two of them, their bond, and the magic that connected them.

As they lay together, wrapped in each other's arms, Elara knew that their journey was just beginning. The path ahead was filled with challenges and mysteries, but with Kael by her side, she felt ready to face whatever came their way.

The night was filled with the sounds of the forest, a symphony of life and magic. Elara closed her eyes, feeling the gentle rise and fall of Kael's chest beneath her head. She felt a deep sense of peace and belonging, knowing that they were connected in a way that transcended time and space.

Their journey had just begun, but Elara knew that with Kael by her side, they could face anything. Together, they would explore the depths of their desires, unlock the true potential of their magic, and forge a bond that would withstand the test of time.

As she drifted off to sleep, Elara felt a warmth spread through her, a promise of the adventures and discoveries that awaited them. And in that moment, she knew that they were exactly where they were meant to be—together, in the enchanted heart of the forest, bound by magic and love.

Chapter 5: Trials of the Heart

Morning light filtered through the trees, casting a soft glow over the glade. Elara awoke with Kael's warmth beside her, the events of the previous day still vivid in her mind. The Enchanted Forest had revealed its wonders, and their bond had grown stronger, but she knew their journey was far from over.

Kael stirred, his eyes opening to meet hers. A soft smile played on his lips, and he brushed a strand of hair away from her face. "Good morning, Elara," he whispered, his voice still husky from sleep.

"Good morning, Kael," she replied, her heart swelling with affection. She reached out and took his hand, savoring the connection between them.

As they prepared to continue their journey, Kael explained the next step in their training. "Today, we will face the Trials of the Heart. These trials are designed to test our control over our desires and emotions. They will challenge us in ways we've never experienced before."

Elara nodded, her determination unwavering. She knew that mastering these trials was essential to harnessing the full potential of their magic.

They ventured deeper into the forest, the air growing cooler and the light dimmer. The path ahead was shrouded in mist, adding an air of mystery and anticipation. Elara felt a sense of trepidation mixed with excitement, knowing that each step brought them closer to the unknown.

At the heart of the forest, they reached a clearing where a circle of ancient stones stood, each one inscribed with runes that pulsed with a faint, otherworldly light. Kael stepped forward, his presence commanding and confident.

"These stones will guide us through the trials," he explained. "Each trial will test a different aspect of our bond. We must remain focused and trust in each other."

Elara took a deep breath and nodded. "I'm ready, Kael. Let's do this together."

Kael placed his hand on the first stone, and a wave of energy rippled through the air. The clearing transformed, becoming a lush, vibrant garden filled with exotic flowers and intoxicating scents. The atmosphere was charged with a palpable sensuality, and Elara could feel her heart race in response.

The first trial began with a challenge to their self-control. The garden seemed to amplify their desires, the air thick with temptation. Elara could feel the pull of the magic, urging her to surrender to the sensations. But she focused on Kael, drawing strength from his presence.

Kael moved closer, his eyes locked onto hers. "Elara, remember your training. Feel the energy, but do not let it overwhelm you."

Elara nodded, closing her eyes and concentrating on the flow of magic within her. She could feel the heat building, the fire of desire threatening to consume her. But with Kael's guidance, she managed to channel it, transforming the raw energy into controlled power.

Their connection grew stronger with each passing moment, their bond a beacon of light amidst the sensual haze. Elara felt Kael's touch, gentle yet electrifying, guiding her through the trial. His hands brushed against her skin, sending shivers of pleasure down her spine.

"You're doing well," Kael whispered, his breath warm against her ear. "Stay focused."

Elara opened her eyes, meeting his gaze. The intensity of his stare sent a thrill through her, but she held her ground, determined to master the trial. They moved together, their movements synchronized, their energies intertwined.

As the trial progressed, the garden seemed to respond to their control. The flowers glowed brighter, their scents becoming more harmonious. Elara could feel the magic weaving around them, a tapestry of desire and power.

Finally, the energy reached a crescendo, and the garden began to fade, the trial coming to an end. Elara and Kael stood together, their breathing heavy, their bodies humming with the residual magic.

"You did it, Elara," Kael said, his voice filled with pride. "You mastered the first trial."

Elara smiled, a sense of accomplishment washing over her. "Thank you, Kael. I couldn't have done it without you."

They moved to the next stone, and Kael placed his hand on its surface. The clearing shifted again, this time transforming into a serene, moonlit lake. The water sparkled like diamonds, and the air was filled with the soothing sound of gentle waves.

The second trial tested their ability to trust and support each other. As they approached the lake, Elara felt a sense of calm wash over her. The magic here was different, softer and more introspective.

Kael led her to the edge of the water, his touch reassuring. "This trial is about trust, Elara. We must rely on each other completely."

Elara nodded, her heart swelling with affection for Kael. "I trust you, Kael. Completely."

They stepped into the lake, the water cool and refreshing against their skin. As they waded deeper, Elara felt a sense of weightlessness, the magic lifting her spirits. She could feel Kael's presence beside her, a steady anchor in the serene landscape.

The water seemed to respond to their emotions, reflecting their trust and connection. Elara felt a surge of warmth as Kael's hand found hers, their fingers intertwining. The simple touch sent a wave of comfort through her, a reminder that they were in this together.

As they reached the center of the lake, the water began to glow, casting a soft, ethereal light around them. Elara could feel the magic enveloping them, a cocoon of trust and intimacy.

"Elara," Kael whispered, his voice carrying across the water. "Trust me."

Elara met his gaze, her heart full. "I trust you, Kael."

With that, Kael pulled her closer, their bodies pressed together in the moonlit water. The sensation was both exhilarating and soothing, a perfect balance of desire and trust. Elara could feel the magic weaving around them, amplifying their connection.

As they stood together, the water swirling around them, Elara felt a deep sense of peace. She knew that they had passed the second trial, their trust in each other unshakeable.

The lake began to fade, the trial coming to an end. Elara and Kael stood on solid ground once more, their bond stronger than ever.

"You did it, Elara," Kael said, his voice filled with admiration. "You trusted me, and we succeeded."

Elara smiled, her heart overflowing with love and gratitude. "I couldn't have done it without you, Kael."

They approached the final stone, the air thick with anticipation. Kael placed his hand on the stone, and the clearing transformed once more, this time into a grand hall filled with mirrors.

The final trial was a test of self-reflection and acceptance. Elara could feel the weight of the challenge, the mirrors reflecting not just their physical forms but their innermost selves.

Kael took her hand, his touch grounding her. "This trial is about seeing ourselves clearly, Elara. We must confront our fears, our desires, and our true selves."

Elara nodded, her resolve firm. "I'm ready, Kael."

As they moved through the hall of mirrors, Elara saw reflections of herself and Kael, each one revealing different aspects of their personalities and emotions. Some mirrors showed their deepest fears, others their greatest desires.

Elara paused in front of a mirror that reflected her doubts and insecurities. She could see the uncertainty in her eyes, the fear of failure. But as she looked deeper, she also saw her strength, her determination, and the love she felt for Kael.

Kael stood beside her, his reflection showing his own struggles and triumphs. Elara could see the weight of his responsibilities, the burden of his past. But she also saw his unwavering dedication, his compassion, and his love for her.

"Elara," Kael said softly, his voice filled with emotion. "We are stronger together. We must accept ourselves and each other, flaws and all."

Elara turned to him, her heart full. "I accept you, Kael. All of you."

Kael smiled, his eyes shining with love. "And I accept you, Elara. All of you."

The mirrors around them glowed with a soft light, reflecting their acceptance and love. Elara could feel the magic weaving around them, a tapestry of self-discovery and connection.

As the final trial came to an end, the hall of mirrors faded, and Elara and Kael stood together in the clearing once more. Their bond had been tested and strengthened, their connection deeper than ever.

"You did it, Elara," Kael said, his voice filled with pride. "You mastered the trials."

Elara smiled, her heart overflowing with love and gratitude. "Thank you, Kael. I couldn't have done it without you."

As they stood together in the clearing, the forest around them seemed to hum with approval, its magic a gentle, protective presence. Elara knew that their journey was far from over, but she felt ready to face whatever came their way.

With Kael by her side, she felt a sense of peace and belonging she had never known. Together, they would explore the depths of their desires, unlock the true potential of their magic, and forge a bond that would withstand the test of time.

Their journey had just begun, and Elara felt a thrill of anticipation as she looked up at Kael, her mentor, her partner, and perhaps, one day, something more. Together, they would face the challenges ahead, their hearts and spirits united by love and magic.

Chapter 6: Secrets of the Past

The moon hung high in the sky, casting a silvery light over the ancient stones of the clearing. Elara and Kael stood together, their hands intertwined, the warmth of their connection a comforting presence in the cool night air. The trials had tested them, but they had emerged stronger, their bond deeper than ever.

As they made their way back to their camp, Kael's hand remained clasped in Elara's, his touch a steady reassurance. The forest seemed to hum with approval, its magic a gentle, protective presence around them. They reached their campsite and settled by the fire, its flickering light casting dancing shadows on their faces.

Kael turned to Elara, his eyes reflecting the firelight. "Elara, there's something I need to share with you," he began, his voice tinged with a hint of vulnerability. "It's about my past."

Elara's heart ached at the uncertainty in his eyes. She reached out and placed her hand on his, squeezing gently. "You can tell me anything, Kael. I'm here for you."

Kael took a deep breath, his gaze locked onto hers. "Many years ago, I loved someone deeply. She was my equal in magic, my partner in every way. But our bond was too intense, our magic too powerful. It consumed us, and in the end, it destroyed her."

Elara felt a pang of sorrow for the pain Kael had endured. She could see the weight of his past in his eyes, the burden of loss he carried. "Kael, I'm so sorry," she whispered, her voice filled with compassion.

Kael's hand tightened around hers. "It's not your fault, Elara. But I need you to understand the dangers we face. Our bond is strong, and our magic is powerful. We must be careful not to let it consume us."

Elara nodded, her heart swelling with determination. "I understand, Kael. We'll face this together, and we won't let our magic control us."

Kael's eyes softened, a small smile playing on his lips. "Thank you, Elara. Your strength and trust mean more to me than you know."

As they sat by the fire, Elara felt a deep yearning to comfort Kael, to show him that he was not alone. She shifted closer, her body brushing against his, the warmth of their connection igniting a spark of desire within her.

Kael's breath hitched, his gaze darkening with an intensity that sent shivers down Elara's spine. "Elara," he murmured, his voice a low, sensual growl. "You have no idea what you do to me."

Elara's heart raced, her own desire mirrored in Kael's eyes. She leaned in, her lips hovering just inches from his. "Show me," she whispered, her voice trembling with anticipation.

Kael's hands moved to her waist, pulling her closer until their bodies were pressed together. The heat between them was palpable, a burning flame that threatened to consume them both. Elara could feel the hard planes of Kael's body against hers, every touch sending waves of pleasure through her.

Their lips met in a searing kiss, a fusion of passion and longing that took Elara's breath away. Kael's hands roamed over her back, his touch firm and possessive, igniting every nerve in her body. Elara's fingers tangled in his hair, pulling him closer, deepening the kiss.

Kael broke the kiss, his breath ragged, his eyes dark with desire. "Elara, we need to be careful," he whispered, though his hands continued to caress her skin, tracing patterns of fire along her spine.

Elara nodded, her own breath coming in short gasps. "I know, Kael. But right now, all I want is you."

Kael groaned softly, his lips finding the sensitive spot on her neck, kissing and nipping gently. Elara's head fell back, a soft moan escaping her lips as she surrendered to the sensations. Kael's hands slid under her tunic, the warmth of his touch against her bare skin sending jolts of pleasure through her.

As their kisses deepened, their movements became more urgent, their desire a blazing fire that threatened to consume them. Elara could feel the magic between them, a pulsing energy that amplified every touch, every kiss. It was a heady mix of passion and power, a tantalizing blend that left her craving more.

Kael's lips traveled down her neck, his hands exploring the curves of her body with a reverence that made Elara's heart swell. She could feel his breath against her skin, each exhale a whisper of desire that sent shivers down her spine. Her own hands roamed over Kael's chest, feeling the strength and warmth beneath his clothes.

"Elara," Kael murmured, his voice a husky caress. "You are everything to me."

Elara's heart skipped a beat at his words, her own feelings mirrored in his eyes. "And you are everything to me, Kael," she replied, her voice trembling with emotion.

Their lips met again, a slow, sensual kiss that conveyed all the longing and love they felt for each other. Kael's hands slid lower, teasing the edge of her tunic, his touch both gentle and possessive. Elara arched into him, her body responding to his every touch, her desire a palpable force.

As their kisses grew more intense, Kael pulled back, his eyes filled with a mixture of love and restraint. "Elara, we need to stop before we go too far."

Elara nodded, her breath coming in short gasps. "I know, Kael. But it's so hard to resist."

Kael's hands cupped her face, his thumbs brushing over her cheeks. "I know, my love. But we must control our desires, not let them control us."

Elara took a deep breath, her heart still racing. "You're right, Kael. We need to be strong."

Kael smiled, his eyes filled with admiration. "You are strong, Elara. And together, we are unstoppable."

They held each other close, the firelight casting a warm glow over their entwined bodies. The intensity of their connection was undeniable, a force that bound them together in ways they had never imagined. Elara could feel the magic between them, a living, breathing presence that amplified their every emotion.

As they lay together, wrapped in each other's arms, Elara felt a deep sense of peace and belonging. She knew that their journey was far from over, but she was ready to face whatever challenges lay ahead. With Kael by her side, she felt a strength and confidence that filled her with hope.

The night passed in a blur of whispered words and tender touches, their bond growing stronger with each passing moment. Elara could feel the weight of Kael's past lifting, the pain of his loss easing in the light of their love.

As dawn broke, casting a golden light over the forest, Elara and Kael rose, their hearts filled with determination. They had faced the trials and emerged stronger, their connection deeper and more profound. Together, they would continue their journey, exploring the depths of their desires and unlocking the true potential of their magic.

With Kael by her side, Elara felt ready to face whatever came their way. Their bond was unbreakable, their love a force that transcended time and space. And as they walked hand in hand through the forest, Elara knew that they were destined for greatness, their hearts and souls intertwined in a dance of love and magic.

Chapter 7: The Seductive Masquerade

The grand hall of the Queen's palace glittered with opulence, its high ceilings adorned with intricate chandeliers that cast a soft, golden glow over the gathering. The masquerade ball was in full swing, the air filled with the hum of music and the gentle murmur of conversation. Guests in elaborate masks and sumptuous gowns danced gracefully across the floor, their movements a tapestry of color and elegance.

Elara stood at the edge of the room, her eyes wide with wonder. She wore a flowing gown of deep sapphire, its fabric shimmering in the candlelight. Her mask, adorned with delicate feathers and gemstones, concealed her features but could not hide the excitement in her eyes. Beside her, Kael cut a striking figure in his tailored suit, his own mask lending him an air of mystery and allure.

As they entered the ballroom, Kael leaned in close, his breath warm against her ear. "Remember, Elara, tonight is not just about the festivities. We need to gather information about the rival sorceress."

Elara nodded, her heart racing with a mix of anticipation and nervousness. The rival sorceress, Lyria, was known for her beauty and cunning, and Elara could feel her presence like a dark shadow in the room. But tonight was also an opportunity for her and Kael to explore their connection in a setting filled with magic and intrigue.

Kael took her hand, guiding her onto the dance floor. The touch of his fingers sent a jolt of electricity through her, and she felt her breath hitch in response. As they moved in perfect synchrony, Elara could feel the heat between them, a simmering tension that had been building for days.

"You're doing beautifully," Kael murmured, his voice a velvety caress. His hand rested lightly on her waist, guiding her effortlessly through the steps of the dance.

Elara's heart swelled with emotion, her senses heightened by the closeness of his body. She could feel the strength in his arms, the warmth of his skin through the fabric of his suit. Every brush of his hand, every glance, seemed to ignite a fire within her, a burning desire that was impossible to ignore.

As the dance continued, Kael's touch became more intimate, his fingers brushing the small of her back, his breath warm against her neck. Elara felt herself melting into his embrace, her body responding to his every move. She could feel the magic between them, a palpable energy that thrummed in the air, binding them together in a dance of desire.

"Kael," she whispered, her voice trembling with longing. "I can't resist you."

Kael's eyes darkened with a mixture of desire and restraint. "We must be careful, Elara," he replied, his voice a husky whisper. "But tonight, let us savor this moment."

Elara's pulse quickened as Kael's hand slid lower, his touch sending shivers of pleasure through her. She felt herself being drawn closer to him, their bodies moving in perfect harmony. The music swelled around them, a sensuous melody that seemed to echo the beating of their hearts.

As the dance came to an end, Kael led Elara to a secluded alcove, hidden from the prying eyes of the other guests. The air was charged with anticipation, the flickering candlelight casting a warm glow over their faces. Kael's hand cupped her cheek, his thumb brushing lightly over her lips.

"Elara," he murmured, his voice thick with emotion. "You are the most beautiful woman here."

Elara felt a flush rise to her cheeks, her heart pounding in her chest. "And you are the most captivating man," she replied, her voice barely above a whisper.

Kael's eyes smoldered with desire as he leaned in, his lips hovering just inches from hers. "I want you," he whispered, his breath warm against her skin.

Elara's breath caught in her throat, her body trembling with anticipation. "I want you too, Kael."

Their lips met in a searing kiss, a fusion of passion and longing that took Elara's breath away. Kael's hands roamed over her body, exploring the curves and contours with a reverence that made her heart swell. She clung to him, her fingers digging into his shoulders as the fire of their desire burned brighter.

Kael's lips trailed down her neck, his kisses sending waves of pleasure through her. Elara arched into him, her body responding to his every touch, her senses alive with the magic of their connection. She could feel the strength of his desire, the depth of his emotions, and it fueled her own longing.

As their kisses grew more intense, Kael pulled back, his eyes dark with desire. "Elara, we must be careful," he whispered, though his hands continued to caress her skin, tracing patterns of fire along her body.

Elara nodded, her breath coming in short gasps. "I know, Kael. But it's so hard to resist."

Kael's hands slid to her waist, pulling her closer until their bodies were pressed together. "We must control our desires, not let them control us," he murmured, his lips brushing against her ear.

Elara shivered at his words, her body aching for his touch. "Yes, Kael," she whispered, her voice trembling with emotion. "I trust you."

Kael's eyes softened, a small smile playing on his lips. "And I trust you, Elara. Together, we are stronger."

They held each other close, the heat of their connection a comforting presence in the cool night air. Elara could feel the magic between them, a living, breathing entity that amplified their every emotion. She knew that their journey was far from over, but she was ready to face whatever challenges lay ahead with Kael by her side.

As they stood together in the secluded alcove, their hearts and spirits united by love and magic, Elara felt a deep sense of peace and belonging. She knew that their bond was unbreakable, their connection a force that transcended time and space. And as they walked hand in hand back into the grand hall, Elara knew that they were destined for greatness, their hearts and souls intertwined in a dance of love and desire.

Chapter 8: A Rival's Touch

The masquerade ball had been a night of enchantment, filled with moments that lingered in Elara's mind long after the last dance ended. The warmth of Kael's touch, the intensity of his gaze, the whispered promises—it was a night she would never forget. But as dawn broke over the horizon, the reality of their mission came crashing back.

The Queen had invited them to a private audience, a rare honor that spoke volumes about the importance of their presence. Elara and Kael walked through the palace corridors, their footsteps echoing off the marble floors. Elara's heart pounded with anticipation and unease, knowing that their mission was not just about collecting ingredients but also about gathering information on their rival, Lyria.

As they entered the grand chamber, the Queen's regal presence commanded the room. She sat on her throne, her eyes sharp and discerning as she regarded them. "Welcome, Elara and Kael," she said, her voice melodic yet authoritative. "I trust the masquerade was to your liking?"

"It was, Your Majesty," Kael replied, bowing respectfully. "We are honored by your invitation."

The Queen nodded, her gaze shifting to Elara. "I have heard much about your skills, Elara. It is rare to see such a powerful bond between a sorceress and her mentor."

Elara felt a blush rise to her cheeks. "Thank you, Your Majesty. It is an honor to be here."

The Queen's eyes narrowed slightly. "I must warn you, Lyria is not one to be underestimated. She is cunning and will stop at nothing to achieve her goals. You must be vigilant."

Kael nodded, his expression serious. "We will be careful, Your Majesty. We appreciate your warning."

The Queen dismissed them with a wave of her hand, and they made their way back through the palace corridors. As they walked, Elara felt a sense of foreboding. She knew that Lyria was dangerous, but hearing it from the Queen herself made it all the more real.

That evening, they decided to explore the palace gardens, hoping to find a moment of respite before their next move. The gardens were a labyrinth of flowers and fountains, the air filled with the scent of blooming roses. Elara and Kael walked hand in hand, the tension of the day melting away in the tranquility of the garden.

As they reached a secluded alcove, Kael turned to Elara, his eyes dark with desire. "Elara," he murmured, his voice a low rumble that sent shivers down her spine. "We need to be careful, but I can't deny my feelings any longer."

Elara's heart raced, her body responding to the heat in his gaze. "Neither can I, Kael," she whispered, stepping closer to him. "I want you."

Kael's hands slid around her waist, pulling her against him. The warmth of his body, the strength of his arms, it all ignited a fire within her. Their lips met in a searing kiss, a fusion of passion and longing that left her breathless. Kael's hands roamed over her back, his touch both gentle and possessive, sending waves of pleasure through her.

"Elara," Kael whispered, his breath hot against her ear. "You drive me wild."

Elara's fingers tangled in his hair, her body arching into his touch. "Kael," she moaned softly, her voice trembling with desire. "Don't stop."

Kael's lips traveled down her neck, his kisses leaving a trail of fire in their wake. Elara's hands explored the hard planes of his chest, feeling the rapid beat of his heart beneath her fingertips. The garden seemed to disappear around them, leaving only the two of them, their connection a blazing inferno of need.

Kael's hands slid lower, caressing the curve of her hips, pulling her even closer. Elara could feel the strength of his desire, the depth of his emotions, and it fueled her own longing. She pressed her body against his, the heat between them almost unbearable.

"Elara," Kael murmured, his voice rough with emotion. "We must be careful, but I want you so much."

Elara's breath hitched, her body trembling with the intensity of her feelings. "I want you too, Kael," she whispered, her voice a plea.

Kael's hands cupped her face, his thumbs brushing lightly over her cheeks. "You are everything to me," he said, his voice filled with a fierce tenderness. "But we must control our desires, not let them control us."

Elara nodded, her heart swelling with love and determination. "I trust you, Kael. We'll be strong together."

They held each other close, their breaths mingling, the heat of their connection a comforting presence in the cool night air. Elara could feel the magic between them, a living, breathing entity that amplified their every emotion. She knew that their journey was far from over, but she felt ready to face whatever challenges lay ahead with Kael by her side.

As they walked back through the garden, their hands intertwined, Elara felt a deep sense of peace and belonging. Their bond was unbreakable, their love a force that transcended time and space. And as they faced the challenges ahead, Elara knew that they were destined for greatness, their hearts and souls intertwined in a dance of love and desire.

The next day, their journey took them to the outskirts of the palace, where they hoped to gather more information about Lyria. They ventured into a dense forest, the air thick with the scent of pine and moss. The path was winding and narrow, but Kael's presence beside her gave Elara the strength to press on.

As they walked, they heard a rustling in the underbrush. Elara's heart raced, her senses on high alert. From the shadows emerged a figure, her beauty striking and her eyes filled with a predatory gleam. It was Lyria.

"Well, well, what do we have here?" Lyria purred, her voice a silky caress that sent a chill down Elara's spine. "Elara and Kael, the inseparable duo."

Kael stepped protectively in front of Elara, his eyes narrowed. "What do you want, Lyria?"

Lyria's gaze flicked to Elara, a sly smile curling her lips. "I simply wanted to see the woman who has captured Kael's heart. You must be quite special, Elara."

Elara felt a surge of anger and protectiveness. "Stay away from us, Lyria."

Lyria laughed, the sound like tinkling bells. "Oh, I'm not here to harm you. Quite the opposite. I find your bond... fascinating."

Kael's hand tightened around Elara's. "Leave us, Lyria. We have no interest in your games."

Lyria's eyes gleamed with amusement. "Very well, but remember this, Elara. Kael is a man of many secrets. Be sure you know what you're getting into."

With that, Lyria disappeared into the shadows, leaving Elara and Kael alone in the forest. Elara's heart pounded, her mind racing with questions.

Kael turned to her, his eyes filled with concern. "Are you alright, Elara?"

Elara nodded, though her thoughts were a whirlwind of confusion and doubt. "I'm fine, Kael. But Lyria's words... they trouble me."

Kael's expression softened, and he pulled her into his arms. "Do not let her get into your head, Elara. Our bond is strong, and I will protect you with everything I have."

Elara clung to him, her heart heavy with emotion. "I trust you, Kael. But I need to know that we can face whatever comes our way together."

Kael's lips brushed against her forehead, a tender promise. "We will, Elara. Together, we are unstoppable."

As they stood there, wrapped in each other's arms, the forest around them seemed to hum with approval, its magic a gentle, protective presence. Elara knew that their journey was far from over, but she felt ready to face whatever challenges lay ahead with Kael by her side.

Their love was a force that transcended time and space, a bond that could withstand any test. And as they walked hand in hand through the forest, Elara knew that they were destined for greatness, their hearts and souls intertwined in a dance of love and desire.

Chapter 9: The Alchemist's Lair

The sun had dipped below the horizon by the time Elara and Kael reached the alchemist's lair, a secluded cottage nestled deep within the forest. The air was thick with the scent of herbs and magic, and a soft glow emanated from the windows, casting an inviting light on the path. Elara's heart raced with anticipation, both for the alchemist's wisdom and for the time alone with Kael in this enchanting place.

As they approached the door, Kael's hand rested on the small of Elara's back, sending a shiver of pleasure through her. The touch was intimate, protective, and it ignited a fire within her that she struggled to control. She leaned into him slightly, savoring the warmth of his body against hers.

The alchemist, an elderly woman with a wise and knowing gaze, greeted them at the door. "Welcome, travelers," she said, her voice soothing and melodic. "Come in, and let us see what knowledge we can uncover together."

The interior of the cottage was a labyrinth of shelves filled with potions, elixirs, and ancient tomes. The air was thick with the scent of incense, creating an atmosphere that was both mystical and intoxicating. Elara and Kael followed the alchemist to a cozy sitting area where a fire crackled warmly in the hearth.

"Please, make yourselves comfortable," the alchemist said, gesturing to the plush chairs. "I understand you seek knowledge of powerful magic and perhaps something more."

Elara and Kael exchanged a glance, their connection unspoken but deeply felt. They sat close together, their knees touching, the heat between them almost tangible. The alchemist observed them with a knowing smile.

"It is rare to see such a strong bond between a sorceress and her mentor," the alchemist said, her eyes twinkling. "But I sense there is more than just mentorship here. There is desire, and that can be a powerful source of magic if harnessed correctly."

Elara felt her cheeks flush, her heart pounding with a mixture of excitement and nervousness. "Yes, we have a strong connection," she admitted, her voice barely above a whisper.

The alchemist nodded. "Desire can amplify your powers, but it must be balanced with control and trust. I have something that may help you achieve that balance." She retrieved a small vial filled with a shimmering liquid and handed it to Kael. "This elixir will heighten your senses and strengthen your bond. Use it wisely."

Kael took the vial, his fingers brushing against Elara's as he did so. The touch sent a jolt of electricity through her, and she could see the same desire mirrored in his eyes. "Thank you," he said, his voice husky with emotion.

The alchemist smiled and left them alone, giving them privacy to explore the depths of their connection. Kael uncorked the vial and offered it to Elara. "Shall we?"

Elara nodded, her eyes locked onto his. "Yes, let's do this together."

They each took a sip of the elixir, the liquid cool and refreshing on their tongues. Almost immediately, Elara felt a rush of sensations, her senses heightened to an almost unbearable degree. The warmth of the fire, the softness of the chair, the closeness of Kael—all of it was magnified, creating a heady mix of pleasure and desire.

Kael's hand found hers, his touch sending waves of heat through her body. "Elara," he murmured, his voice a low rumble that sent shivers down her spine. "I can feel everything so intensely."

"Me too," she whispered, her breath coming in short gasps. "It's like our connection is alive."

Kael's fingers trailed up her arm, his touch leaving a trail of fire in its wake. "We need to be careful, but I want to explore this with you."

Elara nodded, her heart pounding. "Yes, Kael. I want that too."

Their lips met in a slow, sensual kiss, the intensity of their emotions amplified by the elixir. Kael's hands roamed over her back, pulling her closer until their bodies were pressed together. Elara could feel the strength of his desire, the depth of his emotions, and it fueled her own longing.

Kael's lips moved to her neck, his kisses sending waves of pleasure through her. Elara's hands tangled in his hair, pulling him closer, deepening the connection. The world around them seemed to disappear, leaving only the two of them, their desire a living, breathing entity.

As their kisses grew more passionate, Kael's hands slid to her waist, his touch both gentle and possessive. Elara arched into him, her body responding to his every move, her senses overwhelmed by the intensity of their connection.

"Elara," Kael whispered, his breath hot against her ear. "You drive me wild."

Elara's breath hitched, her body trembling with desire. "Kael," she moaned softly, her voice filled with longing. "I can't get enough of you."

Kael's hands slid lower, caressing the curve of her hips, pulling her even closer. "We must be careful, but I want you so much," he murmured, his voice thick with emotion.

Elara nodded, her breath coming in short gasps. "I want you too, Kael. More than anything."

They held each other close, their bodies entwined, the heat between them a comforting presence. Elara could feel the magic of the elixir amplifying their connection, heightening every touch, every kiss. She knew they had to be careful, but in this moment, all she wanted was to lose herself in Kael's embrace.

As the night wore on, they explored the depths of their desire, their connection growing stronger with each passing moment. The fire crackled softly in the hearth, casting a warm glow over their entwined bodies. Elara felt a deep sense of peace and belonging, knowing that with Kael by her side, they could face whatever challenges lay ahead.

Their journey was far from over, but Elara felt ready to face it with Kael. Their bond was unbreakable, their love a force that transcended time and space. And as they lay together in the alchemist's lair, Elara knew that they were destined for greatness, their hearts and souls intertwined in a dance of love and desire.

Chapter 10: The Trial of Fire

The sun had just begun to set as Elara and Kael made their way to the Trial of Fire. The path through the forest was illuminated by the fading light, casting long shadows that danced around them. Their hearts were heavy with anticipation and the weight of the trial ahead. This was one of the most challenging tests they would face, both for their magic and their bond.

Kael's hand rested on the small of Elara's back, a gesture of comfort and support. "Are you ready for this?" he asked softly, his eyes searching hers.

Elara nodded, her heart pounding. "As ready as I'll ever be. With you by my side, I know we can face anything."

They reached the clearing where the Trial of Fire would take place. The air was thick with the scent of burning wood and the crackling of flames. A circle of fire encased a stone platform in the center, the heat radiating outward in waves. Elara could feel the magic in the air, a powerful force that both excited and intimidated her.

Kael turned to her, his expression serious. "This trial will test our control and our connection. We need to focus on each other, trust each other completely."

Elara took a deep breath, nodding. "I trust you, Kael. Let's do this together."

They stepped into the circle, the flames rising higher as if acknowledging their presence. The heat was intense, but Elara felt a strange comfort in it, a reminder of the fire that burned within her for Kael. She reached out and took his hand, their fingers intertwining.

The flames seemed to respond to their touch, swirling around them in a dance of heat and light. Elara could feel the magic coursing through her, a potent mix of power and desire. She closed her eyes and focused on Kael, drawing strength from their connection.

Kael's voice was a soothing balm to her heightened senses. "Feel the fire, Elara. Let it flow through you, but do not let it consume you."

Elara nodded, her breath coming in short gasps. She could feel the fire within her, a roaring inferno of desire and power. But she also felt Kael's presence, a steady anchor that kept her grounded. She focused on their bond, on the love and trust they shared.

Kael's hands moved to her waist, pulling her closer. The heat between them was almost unbearable, but Elara welcomed it, reveling in the intensity of their connection. She could feel every touch, every caress, as if her skin were on fire.

"Elara," Kael murmured, his voice thick with emotion. "You are my strength, my desire."

Elara's heart swelled at his words. "And you are mine, Kael. Together, we are unstoppable."

Their lips met in a fierce, passionate kiss, the fire around them responding to their desire. Kael's hands roamed over her back, his touch igniting sparks of pleasure that left her breathless. Elara's fingers tangled in his hair, pulling him closer, deepening the kiss.

Kael's lips traveled down her neck, his kisses leaving a trail of fire in their wake. Elara arched into him, her body trembling with the intensity of her feelings. She could feel the magic between them, a living, breathing entity that amplified their every emotion.

"Kael," she moaned softly, her voice filled with longing. "I need you."

Kael's hands slid lower, caressing the curve of her hips, pulling her even closer. "And I need you, Elara," he whispered, his breath hot against her ear. "More than anything."

They moved together, their bodies a perfect harmony of desire and control. The flames around them roared higher, reflecting the intensity of their connection. Elara could feel the power of the fire, but she was not afraid. With Kael by her side, she felt invincible.

As the trial continued, Elara and Kael faced each challenge with unwavering resolve. The fire tested their limits, pushing them to the brink, but their bond remained strong. They moved as one, their magic and desire intertwined in a dance of power and passion.

By the time the flames began to die down, Elara felt a sense of accomplishment and peace. They had faced the Trial of Fire and emerged stronger, their connection deeper than ever. Kael's arms wrapped around her, holding her close as the last of the flames flickered out.

"We did it," Elara whispered, her voice filled with awe and gratitude. "We faced the fire and came out stronger."

Kael smiled, his eyes shining with pride and love. "Yes, we did. Together."

As they stood in the clearing, the night air cool against their heated skin, Elara knew that their journey was far from over. But with Kael by her side, she felt ready to face whatever challenges lay ahead. Their bond was unbreakable, their love a force that transcended time and space.

And as they walked hand in hand back through the forest, Elara felt a deep sense of peace and belonging. She knew that they were destined for greatness, their hearts and souls intertwined in a dance of love and desire.

Chapter 11: Forbidden Pleasures

The night was still, the air thick with the fragrance of night-blooming jasmine as Elara and Kael returned to their temporary home, a cozy cabin nestled deep within the forest. The firelight from within cast a welcoming glow through the windows, promising warmth and comfort after the rigors of the Trial of Fire.

As they entered the cabin, Kael closed the door behind them and turned to Elara, his eyes reflecting the flickering flames. "You were incredible today," he said softly, his voice filled with admiration. "Your strength and determination never cease to amaze me."

Elara felt a flush of warmth spread through her at his words. "I couldn't have done it without you, Kael. We make each other stronger."

Kael stepped closer, his hand gently cupping her cheek. "Yes, we do," he murmured, his thumb brushing lightly over her skin. The touch sent a shiver of pleasure through her, and she leaned into his hand, savoring the connection between them.

The cabin's interior was bathed in a warm, golden light, the fire crackling softly in the hearth. The atmosphere was intimate and inviting, wrapping them in a cocoon of safety and desire. Elara felt a deep yearning within her, a longing that had been building since their kiss in the garden.

Kael seemed to sense her thoughts, his eyes darkening with a mix of desire and restraint. "Elara," he whispered, his voice husky, "I want to explore this bond between us, to understand it fully. But we must be careful."

Elara nodded, her breath coming in short, shallow gasps. "I know, Kael. But right now, all I want is to be close to you."

Kael's eyes softened, his hand sliding to the back of her neck as he pulled her into a slow, sensual kiss. The world seemed to fade away, leaving only the two of them, their connection a blazing inferno of need and longing. Elara's hands roamed over his chest, feeling the hard planes of muscle beneath his shirt.

Kael's hands moved to her waist, his touch sending waves of heat through her body. He lifted her effortlessly, guiding her to the plush sofa by the fire. They sank into the cushions, their bodies entwined, the heat between them growing with each passing moment.

Elara's fingers tangled in Kael's hair as she deepened the kiss, her body arching into his touch. The feel of his hands on her skin, the warmth of his breath against her neck, it was all so intoxicating. She wanted more, needed more.

"Kael," she moaned softly, her voice trembling with desire. "I can't get enough of you."

Kael's lips trailed down her neck, his kisses igniting a trail of fire. "Elara," he murmured, his voice a low rumble that sent shivers down her spine. "You have no idea what you do to me."

Their movements became more urgent, their need for each other overwhelming. Kael's hands roamed over her body, exploring every curve and contour with a reverence that made her heart swell. Elara's own hands were just as eager, tracing the lines of his muscles, feeling the strength and warmth that radiated from him.

As their kisses grew more passionate, Kael's lips found the sensitive spot just below her ear, sending a jolt of pleasure through her. Elara's breath hitched, her body trembling with the intensity of her emotions. She could feel the magic between them, a living, breathing entity that amplified their every sensation.

"Elara," Kael whispered, his voice thick with emotion. "We must be careful, but I want you so much."

Elara nodded, her eyes locking onto his. "I want you too, Kael. More than anything."

Kael's hands cupped her face, his thumbs brushing lightly over her cheeks. "You are everything to me," he said, his voice filled with a fierce tenderness. "But we must control our desires, not let them control us."

Elara took a deep breath, her heart swelling with love and determination. "I trust you, Kael. We'll be strong together."

They held each other close, their breaths mingling, the heat of their connection a comforting presence in the cool night air. Elara could feel the magic between them, a living, breathing force that amplified their every emotion. She knew that their journey was far from over, but she felt ready to face whatever challenges lay ahead with Kael by her side.

As they lay together on the sofa, wrapped in each other's arms, the firelight casting a warm glow over their entwined bodies, Elara felt a deep sense of peace and belonging. She knew that their bond was unbreakable, their love a force that transcended time and space. And as they faced the challenges ahead, Elara knew that they were destined for greatness, their hearts and souls intertwined in a dance of love and desire.

The night passed in a blur of whispered words and tender touches, their connection deepening with each passing moment. Elara could feel the weight of their journey ahead, but she also felt the strength of their bond, a beacon of light in the darkness.

With Kael by her side, Elara knew they could face anything. Their love was a force of nature, powerful and unyielding, and together, they were unstoppable. As they drifted off to sleep in each other's arms, Elara knew that whatever challenges lay ahead, they would face them together, their hearts and souls united by love and magic.

Chapter 12: The Dark Sorceress

The first light of dawn filtered through the cabin's windows, casting a soft, golden glow over Elara and Kael as they lay entwined on the sofa. The warmth of their connection lingered in the air, a comforting reminder of the bond they shared. But as the morning light grew stronger, so did the reality of their mission. Today, they would face their greatest challenge yet: confronting the dark sorceress, Lyria.

Elara and Kael prepared in silence, their movements synchronized as they gathered their supplies and readied themselves for the journey ahead. The weight of their task hung heavy in the air, but so did their determination. They had come too far to turn back now.

"Are you ready?" Kael asked, his eyes searching Elara's.

Elara nodded, her heart pounding with a mix of fear and resolve. "Yes, Kael. Let's do this together."

They set out into the forest, the path winding through dense trees and overgrown underbrush. The air was thick with the scent of pine and earth, and the silence was broken only by the occasional rustle of leaves. As they walked, Elara could feel the magic in the air, a dark and oppressive force that grew stronger with each step.

Finally, they reached a clearing where Lyria stood waiting. The dark sorceress was as striking as she was menacing, her beauty only adding to her aura of danger. Her eyes gleamed with a predatory light as she regarded Elara and Kael.

"Welcome," Lyria purred, her voice a silky caress that sent a chill down Elara's spine. "I've been expecting you."

Kael stepped forward, his expression hard and determined. "We're here to stop you, Lyria. Your reign of terror ends today."

Lyria laughed, the sound like tinkling bells. "Oh, Kael. You always did have a flair for the dramatic. But you underestimate the power of desire."

Her eyes flicked to Elara, and a sly smile curled her lips. "And you, Elara. So much potential, so much power. It's a shame you're wasting it on him."

Elara's anger flared, her magic responding to her emotions. "I won't let you hurt anyone else, Lyria. Your dark magic ends here."

Lyria's smile widened, and she raised her hands, dark energy crackling around her fingers. "Let's see if you can back up those words."

The battle began with a clash of magical energies, the air crackling with power. Kael and Elara moved in perfect synchrony, their combined magic creating a formidable force. But Lyria was powerful, her dark magic a relentless assault that tested their limits.

As the battle raged on, Elara felt a surge of power within her, a force fueled by her love for Kael and her determination to protect those she cared about. She focused on their bond, drawing strength from their connection.

"Kael," she called out, her voice ringing with determination. "We need to combine our powers."

Kael nodded, his eyes filled with trust and resolve. "Together, Elara."

They joined hands, their magic merging into a brilliant light that cut through the darkness. The force of their combined power pushed Lyria back, her expression shifting from confidence to shock.

"No!" Lyria screamed, her dark energy wavering. "This cannot be!"

But it was too late. The power of their love and magic was too strong. With one final surge, they overwhelmed Lyria's defenses, the dark sorceress collapsing to the ground in defeat.

The clearing fell silent, the oppressive darkness lifting as Lyria's magic dissipated. Elara and Kael stood together, their breaths coming in ragged gasps, their bodies trembling with the aftershocks of their power.

"We did it," Elara whispered, her voice filled with awe and relief. "We defeated her."

Kael pulled her into his arms, his embrace a comforting anchor. "Yes, we did. Together."

They stood in the clearing, the morning light breaking through the trees, casting a warm glow over them. The air was filled with the scent of fresh pine and earth, a reminder of the life and beauty that had been restored.

As they made their way back to the cabin, Elara felt a sense of peace and accomplishment. They had faced their greatest challenge and emerged stronger, their bond unbreakable. With Kael by her side, she knew they could face whatever lay ahead.

The cabin welcomed them back with its warmth and comfort, the fire crackling softly in the hearth. Elara and Kael sank onto the sofa, their bodies entwined, their hearts full.

"We did it," Elara said softly, her head resting on Kael's chest. "We really did it."

Kael smiled, his fingers gently stroking her hair. "Yes, we did. And we'll face whatever comes next, together."

As they lay together, wrapped in each other's arms, Elara felt a deep sense of belonging. Their journey was far from over, but she knew that with Kael by her side, they could overcome any obstacle. Their love was a force of nature, powerful and unyielding, and together, they were unstoppable.

As the firelight cast a warm glow over their entwined bodies, Elara closed her eyes, feeling the steady beat of Kael's heart beneath her ear. She knew that whatever challenges lay ahead, they would face them together, their hearts and souls united by love and magic. And as she drifted off to sleep in Kael's arms, Elara knew that they were destined for greatness, their bond a beacon of light in the darkness.

Chapter 13: The Queen's Favor

The following morning, the sun rose bright and clear over Elysia, casting its warm rays over the land. Elara and Kael had barely slept, their minds still buzzing from the intense battle and their hearts filled with the triumph of their victory. They knew they had to return to the Queen and report their success.

As they made their way back to the palace, hand in hand, the forest seemed to come alive around them, a reflection of their own renewed spirits. Birds sang a joyful chorus, and the air was filled with the sweet scent of blooming flowers. Elara felt a deep sense of peace and satisfaction, knowing that they had not only defeated Lyria but had also grown stronger together.

The palace guards greeted them with respectful bows as they approached the grand entrance. Word of their victory had already spread, and they were welcomed as heroes. The Queen awaited them in her throne room, her regal presence commanding the space.

"Elara, Kael," she said, her voice filled with warmth and admiration. "You have done a great service to Elysia. The threat of Lyria is no more, thanks to your bravery and skill."

Elara and Kael bowed deeply. "It was an honor to serve, Your Majesty," Kael replied.

The Queen's eyes softened as she looked at them. "I can see that your bond has grown even stronger through this ordeal. Such a connection is rare and precious. As a token of my gratitude, I would like to grant you both a boon. Ask for anything within my power, and it shall be yours."

Elara and Kael exchanged a glance, their thoughts aligned. "Your Majesty," Elara began, her voice steady. "We wish to continue our studies and our journey together. We ask for access to the Royal Archives and the resources to explore the ancient magics that will help us protect Elysia."

The Queen smiled, clearly pleased with their request. "You shall have it. The Royal Archives are at your disposal, and you will be provided with whatever you need for your journey. May your bond and your magic continue to grow and bring light to our land."

With their boon granted, Elara and Kael spent the next several days delving into the Royal Archives. The vast collection of ancient tomes and scrolls was a treasure trove of knowledge, and they eagerly absorbed everything they could. Each discovery brought them closer together, their minds and hearts intertwined in their quest for understanding and mastery.

One evening, after hours of intense study, Kael suggested they take a break and explore the palace gardens. The moon was high in the sky, casting a silvery light over the carefully tended flowers and winding pathways. The cool night air was refreshing, and Elara felt her spirits lift as they wandered hand in hand through the serene landscape.

They reached a secluded gazebo, its white pillars draped with fragrant jasmine. The intimate setting, bathed in moonlight, seemed to beckon them closer. Kael led Elara to a cushioned bench, where they sat together, the world around them fading away.

"Elara," Kael said softly, his eyes reflecting the moonlight. "These past days have been incredible, but I realize we haven't had a moment to truly celebrate our victory and our bond."

Elara's heart swelled with love and gratitude. "You're right, Kael. We've been so focused on our studies that we haven't taken the time to just be together."

Kael's hand found hers, his touch sending a familiar warmth through her. "Let's take this moment now," he murmured, his voice filled with tenderness.

Their lips met in a slow, passionate kiss, the intensity of their emotions flowing between them. Elara felt a surge of desire, her body responding to Kael's touch with a longing that had been building for days. His hands caressed her back, pulling her closer, deepening their connection.

"Kael," she whispered, her breath coming in short gasps. "I want to be close to you, to feel you."

Kael's eyes darkened with desire, his hand sliding to the back of her neck. "I feel the same, Elara. I want to explore every part of you, to show you how much you mean to me."

Their kisses grew more urgent, their hands exploring each other's bodies with a fervor that left them both breathless. Elara could feel the heat between them, a fire that threatened to consume her. But she welcomed it, reveling in the intensity of their connection.

Kael's lips traveled down her neck, his kisses igniting a trail of fire. Elara's fingers tangled in his hair, pulling him closer, deepening the kiss. She could feel the strength of his desire, the depth of his emotions, and it fueled her own longing.

"Elara," Kael murmured against her skin, his voice a husky whisper. "You drive me wild."

Elara's breath hitched, her body trembling with desire. "Kael," she moaned softly, her voice filled with longing. "I can't get enough of you."

Kael's hands roamed over her body, his touch both gentle and possessive. "We must be careful, but I want you so much," he murmured, his breath hot against her ear.

Elara nodded, her breath coming in short gasps. "I want you too, Kael. More than anything."

They held each other close, their bodies entwined, the heat between them a comforting presence in the cool night air. Elara could feel the magic between them, a living, breathing entity that amplified their every emotion. She knew that their journey was far from over, but she felt ready to face whatever challenges lay ahead with Kael by her side.

As they lay together in the gazebo, wrapped in each other's arms, the moonlight casting a soft glow over their entwined bodies, Elara felt a deep sense of peace and belonging. She knew that their bond was unbreakable, their love a force that transcended time and space. And as they faced the challenges ahead, Elara knew that they were destined for greatness, their hearts and souls intertwined in a dance of love and desire.

The night passed in a blur of whispered words and tender touches, their connection deepening with each passing moment. Elara could feel the weight of their journey ahead, but she also felt the strength of their bond, a beacon of light in the darkness.

With Kael by her side, Elara knew they could face anything. Their love was a force of nature, powerful and unyielding, and together, they were unstoppable. As they drifted off to sleep in each other's arms, Elara knew that whatever challenges lay ahead, they would face them together, their hearts and souls united by love and magic.

Chapter 14: The Spell of Binding

The days that followed were filled with intense study and preparation. Elara and Kael immersed themselves in the Royal Archives, uncovering secrets of ancient magic that would aid them in their quest to protect Elysia. The knowledge they gained was vast, but one spell stood out among the rest—a binding spell that would unite their powers in a way that transcended individual strength.

Elara felt a mixture of excitement and apprehension as they prepared to perform the spell. It was a ritual that required absolute trust and synchronization, a melding of their very essences. She could sense the weight of the spell, its importance, and the potential consequences if not executed perfectly.

"Are you sure about this, Kael?" Elara asked, her voice steady but tinged with uncertainty.

Kael looked at her, his eyes filled with unwavering determination. "Elara, we've come this far together. This spell will not only strengthen our magic but also solidify our bond. I trust you completely."

Elara nodded, taking a deep breath. "I trust you too, Kael. Let's do this."

They chose a secluded grove within the palace gardens for the ritual. The space was serene and filled with the soft glow of moonlight filtering through the trees. The air was thick with the scent of blooming flowers, creating an atmosphere that was both mystical and intimate.

Kael arranged the components for the spell—crystals, candles, and a mixture of rare herbs they had gathered. Elara stood beside him, feeling the energy in the air grow stronger with each passing moment. They had spent days perfecting the incantations and the precise movements required for the ritual.

As they stood in the center of the grove, Kael took Elara's hands in his, his touch sending a familiar warmth through her. "Elara, this spell is about more than just magic. It's about us, our connection, and our commitment to each other."

Elara felt a surge of emotion, her heart swelling with love and determination. "I'm ready, Kael. Let's begin."

They closed their eyes, focusing on the energy between them. Kael began to chant the incantation, his voice low and resonant, blending with the natural sounds of the grove. Elara joined in, their voices harmonizing in a way that felt both powerful and intimate.

The candles around them flickered to life, casting a warm, golden light. The crystals glowed with an inner radiance, reflecting the magic they were channeling. Elara could feel the energy building, a potent mix of power and desire that thrummed through her veins.

As the incantation reached its peak, Kael's grip on her hands tightened, and she opened her eyes to find his gaze locked onto hers. The intensity in his eyes mirrored her own feelings, a blend of love, determination, and desire.

"Elara," Kael whispered, his voice filled with emotion. "This spell will bind us together in ways we can't even imagine. Are you ready?"

Elara nodded, her heart pounding. "Yes, Kael. I'm ready."

The final words of the incantation left their lips, and a brilliant light enveloped them, the magic of the spell weaving around their bodies. Elara could feel the bond strengthening, their powers merging into a single, unstoppable force. It was a sensation unlike any other, a deep connection that transcended the physical.

Kael's hands slid to her waist, pulling her closer. The warmth of his body, the strength of his embrace, it all amplified the intensity of the moment. Their lips met in a searing kiss, a fusion of their magic and their love. Elara felt a rush of sensations, her body responding to Kael's touch with a longing that left her breathless.

"Elara," Kael murmured against her lips, his voice thick with desire. "I can feel our bond growing stronger."

Elara's fingers tangled in his hair, pulling him closer. "So can I, Kael. It's incredible."

Their kisses grew more passionate, their bodies moving in perfect harmony. The magic of the binding spell thrummed around them, heightening every touch, every caress. Elara could feel the energy between them, a living, breathing entity that amplified their connection.

Kael's lips trailed down her neck, his kisses igniting a trail of fire. Elara's breath hitched, her body trembling with the intensity of her feelings. She could feel the strength of their bond, the depth of their emotions, and it fueled her own longing.

"Kael," she moaned softly, her voice filled with longing. "I need you."

Kael's hands roamed over her body, his touch both gentle and possessive. "And I need you, Elara," he whispered, his breath hot against her ear. "More than anything."

They held each other close, their bodies entwined, the heat between them a comforting presence in the cool night air. Elara could feel the magic of the binding spell weaving around them, a living, breathing force that amplified their every emotion. She knew that their journey was far from over, but she felt ready to face whatever challenges lay ahead with Kael by her side.

As they lay together in the grove, wrapped in each other's arms, the moonlight casting a soft glow over their entwined bodies, Elara felt a deep sense of peace and belonging. She knew that their bond was unbreakable, their love a force that transcended time and space. And as they faced the challenges ahead, Elara knew that they were destined for greatness, their hearts and souls intertwined in a dance of love and desire.

The night passed in a blur of whispered words and tender touches, their connection deepening with each passing moment. Elara could feel the weight of their journey ahead, but she also felt the strength of their bond, a beacon of light in the darkness.

With Kael by her side, Elara knew they could face anything. Their love was a force of nature, powerful and unyielding, and together, they were unstoppable. As they drifted off to sleep in each other's arms, Elara knew that whatever challenges lay ahead, they would face them together, their hearts and souls united by love and magic.

Chapter 15: Night of the Full Moon

The moon hung high in the sky, casting a silvery glow over the forest as Elara and Kael prepared for the final binding ritual. This night was special—the full moon amplified their magic, making it the perfect time to solidify their bond and harness the full power of their connection.

They stood in a secluded clearing, the air thick with anticipation and the scent of blooming flowers. The magic of the full moon was palpable, a soft hum that resonated through their bodies. Elara felt her heart race with a mixture of excitement and nervousness. Tonight was the culmination of all their efforts, a night that would change their lives forever.

Kael turned to her, his eyes reflecting the moonlight. "Elara, are you ready?"

Elara nodded, her voice steady despite the butterflies in her stomach. "Yes, Kael. I'm ready."

They had spent days preparing for this moment, gathering rare ingredients and perfecting the incantations. The clearing was adorned with a circle of candles, their flames flickering gently in the night breeze. In the center, a crystal altar held the key components for the ritual—a vial of elixir, a binding talisman, and a sacred scroll.

Kael took Elara's hand, his touch sending a familiar warmth through her. "Remember, this ritual is not just about our magic. It's about our commitment to each other, our trust, and our love."

Elara's heart swelled with emotion. "I understand, Kael. Let's do this together."

They began the ritual, their voices harmonizing as they chanted the ancient incantations. The air around them seemed to shimmer with magic, the candles' flames growing brighter with each word. Elara could feel the energy building, a potent mix of power and desire that thrummed through her veins.

Kael uncorked the vial of elixir and offered it to Elara. She took a sip, the liquid cool and refreshing on her tongue, and then handed it back to him. Kael drank deeply, their eyes locking as they shared the elixir. The sensation was immediate—a rush of heightened senses, an intense connection that left them both breathless.

Kael placed the binding talisman around Elara's neck, the cool metal warming instantly against her skin. The talisman glowed with an inner light, reflecting the magic of their bond. Elara felt a surge of power, her magic and Kael's intertwining in a dance of light and energy.

"Elara," Kael whispered, his voice filled with reverence and desire. "You are my heart, my strength, my everything."

Tears filled Elara's eyes as she looked at him. "And you are mine, Kael. I love you more than words can express."

Their lips met in a slow, passionate kiss, the magic around them amplifying their emotions. Kael's hands roamed over her back, pulling her closer, deepening their connection. Elara could feel the heat between them, a fire that burned brighter with each touch, each caress.

"Kael," she murmured against his lips, her voice trembling with desire. "I need you."

Kael's eyes darkened with a mix of love and longing. "And I need you, Elara."

They moved together, their bodies pressed close, the magic of the ritual heightening every sensation. Kael's lips trailed down her neck, his kisses igniting a trail of fire. Elara's fingers tangled in his hair, pulling him closer, deepening the kiss. She could feel the strength of their bond, the depth of their emotions, and it fueled her own longing.

As the ritual reached its peak, the crystal altar glowed with a brilliant light, the energy of their bond pulsating through the clearing. Elara and Kael chanted the final words of the incantation, their voices merging into one. The binding talisman around Elara's neck grew warm, a tangible symbol of their connection.

"Elara," Kael whispered, his breath hot against her ear. "I can feel our bond strengthening."

Elara's heart pounded with a mixture of love and magic. "So can I, Kael. It's incredible."

They held each other close, their bodies entwined, the heat between them a comforting presence in the cool night air. Elara could feel the magic of the binding spell weaving around them, a living, breathing force that amplified their every emotion. She knew that their journey was far from over, but she felt ready to face whatever challenges lay ahead with Kael by her side.

As they lay together in the clearing, wrapped in each other's arms, the moonlight casting a soft glow over their entwined bodies, Elara felt a deep sense of peace and belonging. She knew that their bond was unbreakable, their love a force that transcended time and space. And as they faced the challenges ahead, Elara knew that they were destined for greatness, their hearts and souls intertwined in a dance of love and desire.

The night passed in a blur of whispered words and tender touches, their connection deepening with each passing moment. Elara could feel the weight of their journey ahead, but she also felt the strength of their bond, a beacon of light in the darkness.

With Kael by her side, Elara knew they could face anything. Their love was a force of nature, powerful and unyielding, and together, they were unstoppable. As they drifted off to sleep in each other's arms, Elara knew that whatever challenges lay ahead, they would face them together, their hearts and souls united by love and magic.

Chapter 16: The Shadow Realm

The dawn after the binding ritual brought with it a renewed sense of purpose and strength. Elara and Kael woke in each other's arms, the warmth of their connection a comforting reminder of the previous night's magic. The binding spell had strengthened their bond, and they both felt a deeper sense of unity and power.

As they prepared for the day, Kael spoke of their next challenge. "Elara, there's one more journey we must undertake to ensure the safety of Elysia. We need to venture into the Shadow Realm to confront the entity that cast the curse on me. Only then can we ensure that no lingering darkness threatens our land."

Elara felt a shiver of apprehension but nodded firmly. "I'm with you, Kael. We will face this together."

They gathered their supplies and set out towards the ancient portal that led to the Shadow Realm. The portal was hidden deep within a cave, its entrance shrouded in darkness. As they approached, Elara felt the oppressive energy of the realm seep through, a stark contrast to the vibrant life of Elysia.

Kael took her hand, his grip reassuring. "Stay close to me, Elara. The Shadow Realm is filled with illusions and temptations. We must rely on our bond to guide us."

Elara nodded, her heart pounding. "I trust you, Kael."

They stepped through the portal, and the world around them shifted. The Shadow Realm was a twisted mirror of Elysia, filled with dark, distorted versions of the familiar landscapes. The air was heavy with a sense of foreboding, and Elara could feel the malevolent presence of the entity watching them.

As they journeyed deeper into the realm, the darkness seemed to close in around them, whispering voices tempting them to stray from their path. Elara felt a flicker of doubt and fear, but Kael's steady presence kept her grounded.

"Remember our bond," Kael murmured, his voice a calming anchor in the sea of darkness. "We are stronger together."

Elara focused on their connection, drawing strength from the love and trust they shared. The whispers grew fainter, the darkness less oppressive, as they moved forward with renewed determination.

Finally, they reached the heart of the Shadow Realm, a vast, empty expanse where the entity awaited. It appeared as a swirling mass of shadows, its form constantly shifting and changing. Its eyes glowed with an eerie light, and its voice echoed through the void.

"Kael, Elara," the entity hissed, its tone mocking. "You think you can defeat me? Your bond is strong, but it will not be enough."

Kael stepped forward, his eyes blazing with determination. "We will defeat you. Our love is stronger than your darkness."

Elara felt a surge of pride and love for Kael, his strength and resolve inspiring her own. She stood beside him, her hand in his, ready to face whatever the entity threw at them.

The entity laughed, its form growing larger and more menacing. "Very well. Let's see if your love can withstand the ultimate test."

The ground beneath them shook, and the darkness intensified. Elara could feel the entity's power pressing down on them, trying to force them apart. She focused on their bond, drawing on the magic of the binding spell and the love they shared.

"Kael," she whispered, her voice filled with determination. "We can do this. Together."

Kael nodded, his grip on her hand tightening. "Together."

They chanted the incantation they had prepared, their voices harmonizing and blending with the magic around them. The light of their bond grew brighter, pushing back the darkness. The entity howled in rage, its form becoming unstable.

"You cannot defeat me!" it shrieked, its voice filled with desperation.

But Elara and Kael pressed on, their love and magic intertwining in a brilliant display of power. The light of their bond pierced through the entity's form, shattering it into a thousand fragments of shadow. The oppressive darkness lifted, and the Shadow Realm began to dissolve around them.

As the realm faded, Elara and Kael found themselves back in the cave, the portal to the Shadow Realm now sealed. They stood together, their breaths coming in ragged gasps, their bodies trembling with the aftershocks of their victory.

"We did it," Elara whispered, her voice filled with awe and relief. "We defeated the entity."

Kael pulled her into his arms, his embrace strong and comforting. "Yes, we did. Together."

They left the cave and made their way back to Elysia, the bright sunlight and vibrant life a stark contrast to the dark realm they had just left. As they walked through the forest, Elara felt a deep sense of peace and accomplishment. They had faced their greatest challenge and emerged stronger, their bond unbreakable.

Back at the palace, they were welcomed as heroes. The Queen herself greeted them, her eyes filled with pride and gratitude. "Elara, Kael, you have saved Elysia from a great darkness. Your bravery and love are an inspiration to us all."

Elara and Kael bowed deeply. "It was our honor, Your Majesty," Kael replied.

The Queen smiled warmly. "Your bond is a testament to the power of love and magic. May it continue to shine brightly and guide us all."

As they stood together, surrounded by the beauty and light of Elysia, Elara knew that their journey was far from over. But with Kael by her side, she felt ready to face whatever challenges lay ahead. Their love was a force of nature, powerful and unyielding, and together, they were unstoppable.

As they walked hand in hand through the palace gardens, the sun setting in a blaze of color, Elara felt a deep sense of peace and belonging. Their hearts and souls were intertwined, their bond a beacon of light in the darkness. And as they looked to the future, Elara knew that they were destined for greatness, their love a guiding force in the magic of Elysia.

Chapter 17: Confronting the Past

The days following their triumph in the Shadow Realm were filled with celebration and newfound peace. Elara and Kael were hailed as heroes, their bond and bravery serving as an inspiration to all of Elysia. But amidst the joy and relief, there was still one task left unfinished—Kael's past.

Kael had shared with Elara the tragic story of his former lover, whose death had cast a long shadow over his heart. Now, with their bond stronger than ever, they felt ready to confront the lingering darkness of his past and lay it to rest.

They traveled to the far reaches of Elysia, to a place where the remnants of Kael's past awaited. It was a serene, hidden glade, filled with the scent of blooming wildflowers and the gentle hum of nature. The air was thick with magic, and Elara could feel its pulsing energy, a mixture of sorrow and hope.

Kael stood at the edge of the glade, his eyes distant as he gazed at the place where his past had unfolded. Elara stepped closer, her hand slipping into his, offering silent support.

"Are you ready, Kael?" Elara asked softly, her voice filled with understanding.

Kael nodded, taking a deep breath. "Yes, Elara. With you by my side, I can face anything."

They moved to the center of the glade, where an ancient oak tree stood as a sentinel of time. Its gnarled branches stretched towards the sky, and beneath its protective canopy lay a small, stone altar. Kael knelt before it, his hands trembling slightly as he placed a delicate, white flower on the altar.

"This is where it happened," Kael said, his voice barely above a whisper. "Where I lost her. I've carried this pain for so long, but now it's time to let it go."

Elara knelt beside him, her hand resting gently on his back. "We'll do this together, Kael. Our bond will guide us."

Kael took her hand, drawing strength from her presence. Together, they began to chant, their voices blending harmoniously, calling upon the magic of the glade to help them release the pain of the past. The air around them shimmered with light, the magic responding to their heartfelt plea.

As they chanted, Elara could feel the warmth of their connection, the bond they had forged growing even stronger. Kael's hand tightened around hers, and she sensed his resolve, his desire to finally find peace. The magic of the glade seemed to wrap around them, creating a cocoon of light and warmth.

"Elara," Kael whispered, his voice filled with emotion. "Thank you for being here with me. I couldn't do this without you."

Elara leaned in, her lips brushing against his in a tender, yet deeply passionate kiss. "I'm always here for you, Kael. Forever."

Their kiss deepened, the intensity of their emotions flowing between them. Elara could feel the heat of their connection, a blazing fire that seemed to burn away the shadows of the past. Kael's hands roamed over her back, pulling her closer, as if seeking comfort and reassurance in her touch.

"Elara," Kael murmured against her lips, his voice thick with desire. "You are my light, my love."

Elara's heart swelled at his words, her own desire mirrored in his eyes. "And you are mine, Kael. Always."

Their kisses grew more urgent, their bodies pressing together in a dance of need and passion. The magic of the glade seemed to amplify every touch, every caress, creating a heady mix of pleasure and power. Elara felt as if they were merging into one, their bond a tangible force that pulsed with life.

Kael's lips trailed down her neck, his kisses igniting a trail of fire. Elara's breath hitched, her body trembling with the intensity of her feelings. She could feel the depth of Kael's love, the strength of their connection, and it fueled her own longing.

"Kael," she moaned softly, her voice filled with yearning. "I need you."

Kael's hands slid to her waist, his touch both gentle and possessive. "And I need you, Elara," he whispered, his breath hot against her ear. "More than anything."

They moved together, their bodies a perfect harmony of desire and control. The light around them brightened, the magic of the glade reaching its peak as they chanted the final words of their spell. A wave of energy surged through them, cleansing away the pain of the past and leaving only the purity of their love.

As the light faded, Elara and Kael found themselves still entwined, their breaths coming in ragged gasps, their bodies humming with the aftershocks of their magic. The glade felt different now, the air lighter, the oppressive weight of sorrow lifted.

"We did it," Kael whispered, his voice filled with awe and relief. "We've finally let go of the past."

Elara smiled, her heart overflowing with love. "Yes, Kael. We did it together."

They sat in the glade for a while longer, basking in the peace and tranquility of the moment. Elara felt a deep sense of contentment, knowing that they had faced one of their greatest challenges and emerged stronger. Their bond was unbreakable, their love a force that transcended time and space.

As they made their way back through the forest, hand in hand, Elara felt a renewed sense of purpose. They had overcome so much together, and she knew that they could face whatever the future held. With Kael by her side, she felt ready to embrace their destiny, their hearts and souls united in a dance of love and magic.

Chapter 18: Rebirth

The dawn after their emotional journey brought a sense of renewal. The forest around them seemed more vibrant, the colors more vivid, the sounds more harmonious. Elara and Kael returned to their cabin, their hearts lighter, their bond even stronger.

As they entered the cabin, the air was filled with the scent of the wildflowers they had gathered the previous day. Elara set the flowers in a vase, the vibrant colors brightening the room. Kael moved to light a fire in the hearth, the flames dancing warmly, casting a golden glow over their cozy haven.

Kael turned to Elara, his eyes dark with desire. "Elara, after everything we've been through, I feel closer to you than ever. Our bond is unbreakable, and I want to celebrate that with you."

Elara felt her heart race, her body responding to the heat in his gaze. "I feel the same, Kael. I want to celebrate us."

Kael crossed the room, his steps deliberate and slow, as if savoring each moment. He took her hands in his, the warmth of his touch sending shivers through her. "Elara," he murmured, his voice a husky whisper. "You are my light, my love, my everything."

Elara's breath hitched, her eyes locked onto his. "And you are mine, Kael. Always."

Their lips met in a slow, passionate kiss, a dance of desire and love that left them both breathless. Kael's hands roamed over her back, pulling her closer, deepening the connection between them. Elara could feel the heat between them, a fire that burned brighter with each touch, each caress.

Kael's lips trailed down her neck, his kisses igniting a trail of fire. Elara's fingers tangled in his hair, pulling him closer, deepening the kiss. She could feel the strength of his desire, the depth of his emotions, and it fueled her own longing.

"Kael," she moaned softly, her voice trembling with need. "I need you."

Kael's hands slid to her waist, his touch both gentle and possessive. "And I need you, Elara," he whispered, his breath hot against her ear. "More than anything."

They moved together, their bodies pressed close, the heat between them almost unbearable. Kael's hands explored every curve and contour of her body, his touch leaving a trail of burning desire in its wake. Elara could feel the magic of their bond amplifying every sensation, every touch, creating a heady mix of pleasure and longing.

"Elara," Kael murmured against her skin, his voice filled with reverence and passion. "You drive me wild."

Elara's breath came in short gasps, her body trembling with the intensity of her feelings. "Kael," she whispered, her voice thick with desire. "I can't get enough of you."

Kael's lips claimed hers once more, the kiss deep and hungry, their bodies moving in perfect harmony. Elara could feel the magic between them, a living, breathing entity that amplified their every emotion. She felt as if they were merging into one, their bond a tangible force that pulsed with life.

As their kisses grew more urgent, Kael's hands found the hem of her tunic, lifting it slowly, reverently, as if unwrapping a precious gift. Elara's skin tingled with anticipation, the cool air contrasting with the heat of his touch. Kael's eyes darkened with desire as he looked at her, his breath coming in ragged gasps.

"Elara," he whispered, his voice trembling with emotion. "You are so beautiful."

Elara felt a blush rise to her cheeks, her heart swelling with love. "And you, Kael, are everything I've ever wanted."

They moved to the bed, their bodies entwined, the heat between them a comforting presence. Kael's hands explored her body with a gentle, yet possessive touch, igniting a fire that burned brighter with each caress. Elara could feel the depth of his love, the strength of their bond, and it fueled her own desire.

"Kael," she moaned softly, her voice filled with longing. "I need you."

Kael's eyes locked onto hers, his gaze filled with a mixture of love and desire. "And I need you, Elara. Always."

They moved together in a dance of love and passion, their bodies and souls entwined. The magic of their bond pulsed around them, amplifying every sensation, every touch, creating a symphony of pleasure and longing. Elara felt as if they were merging into one, their connection a living, breathing entity that pulsed with life.

As the morning light filtered through the window, casting a soft, golden glow over their entwined bodies, Elara felt a deep sense of peace and belonging. They had faced their past, embraced their present, and looked forward to their future, their hearts and souls united by love and magic.

"Kael," she whispered, her voice filled with emotion. "I love you."

Kael's hand cupped her cheek, his eyes shining with love. "And I love you, Elara. Forever."

As they lay together, wrapped in each other's arms, the world outside faded away, leaving only the warmth of their connection, the strength of their bond, and the depth of their love. And as they drifted off to sleep in each other's arms, Elara knew that whatever challenges lay ahead, they would face them together, their hearts and souls intertwined in a dance of love and desire.

Chapter 19: New Beginnings

The days that followed were filled with a sense of serenity and joy. The air seemed sweeter, the sun brighter, and the world more alive. Elara and Kael had not only overcome their greatest challenges but had also deepened their bond in ways they had never imagined. Their love and magic had woven together into a tapestry of strength and unity, and they were ready to embrace the future with renewed vigor.

One morning, as they enjoyed breakfast in the garden of their cabin, Kael turned to Elara, his eyes sparkling with excitement. "Elara, there's something I've been thinking about. Our journey so far has been incredible, but I believe we have more to offer Elysia. What if we established a place where others can come to learn about the magic of love and connection? A sanctuary where bonds like ours can be nurtured and strengthened."

Elara's heart leapt at the idea. "Kael, that's a wonderful idea. We could help so many people discover their true potential and the power of their connections. Let's do it."

They spent the next few weeks planning their sanctuary, envisioning a place filled with light and love, where magic could flourish. They traveled across Elysia, seeking out those who could help them build their dream. Artisans, healers, and fellow sorcerers joined their cause, each adding their unique skills to the creation of the sanctuary.

The sanctuary was nestled in a lush valley, surrounded by mountains that seemed to protect and cradle it. The buildings were crafted from stone and wood, designed to blend seamlessly with the natural beauty of the landscape. Gardens filled with vibrant flowers and herbs surrounded the structures, their scents mingling in the air, creating an atmosphere of peace and tranquility.

As the sanctuary took shape, Elara and Kael worked tirelessly, their bond growing even stronger as they poured their hearts into their creation. They designed spaces for teaching, healing, and meditation, each area infused with their magic and love.

One evening, as they stood together on a hill overlooking the sanctuary, Kael wrapped his arms around Elara, pulling her close. "Elara, look at what we've created. This is more than I ever dreamed possible."

Elara leaned into his embrace, her heart swelling with pride and love. "It's beautiful, Kael. And it's only the beginning. Together, we can make this sanctuary a beacon of hope and love for all of Elysia."

As the sun set, casting a golden glow over the valley, they made their way back to their cabin, hand in hand. The warmth of their connection, the strength of their bond, filled Elara with a deep sense of peace and contentment.

Later that night, they lay together in bed, the soft glow of the fire casting shadows on the walls. Kael's hand gently caressed Elara's back, his touch sending shivers of pleasure through her. "Elara," he murmured, his voice thick with emotion. "You are my everything. I love you more than words can express."

Elara's breath hitched, her body responding to his touch. "And you are my everything, Kael. I love you with all my heart."

Their lips met in a slow, passionate kiss, the intensity of their emotions flowing between them. Kael's hands roamed over her body, his touch both gentle and possessive. Elara could feel the heat between them, a fire that burned brighter with each touch, each caress.

"Kael," she moaned softly, her voice trembling with need. "I need you."

Kael's eyes darkened with desire, his hand sliding to the back of her neck. "And I need you, Elara."

Their kisses grew more urgent, their bodies moving in perfect harmony. The magic of their bond thrummed around them, amplifying every sensation, every touch. Elara felt as if they were merging into one, their connection a living, breathing entity that pulsed with life.

"Elara," Kael whispered against her skin, his voice filled with reverence and passion. "You drive me wild."

Elara's breath came in short gasps, her body trembling with the intensity of her feelings. "Kael," she whispered, her voice thick with desire. "I can't get enough of you."

Kael's lips claimed hers once more, the kiss deep and hungry, their bodies moving together in a dance of love and passion. Elara could feel the magic between them, a living, breathing force that amplified their every emotion. She felt as if they were merging into one, their bond a tangible force that pulsed with life.

As the night wore on, they explored the depths of their desire, their connection growing stronger with each passing moment. The fire crackled softly in the hearth, casting a warm glow over their entwined bodies. Elara felt a deep sense of peace and belonging, knowing that with Kael by her side, they could face anything.

"Kael," she whispered, her voice filled with emotion. "I love you."

Kael's hand cupped her cheek, his eyes shining with love. "And I love you, Elara. Forever."

As they lay together, wrapped in each other's arms, the world outside faded away, leaving only the warmth of their connection, the strength of their bond, and the depth of their love. And as they drifted off to sleep in each other's arms, Elara knew that whatever challenges lay ahead, they would face them together, their hearts and souls united by love and magic.

The sanctuary became a haven for those seeking to understand the magic of love and connection. Under Elara and Kael's guidance, bonds were forged, and lives were transformed. Their legacy grew, their names becoming synonymous with hope and love throughout Elysia.

As they stood together, watching the sunrise over their sanctuary, Elara felt a deep sense of fulfillment. They had created something beautiful, something lasting. And as long as they were together, their love would continue to inspire and guide others.

"Kael," she said softly, her voice filled with emotion. "This is just the beginning."

Kael smiled, his eyes filled with love. "Yes, Elara. Just the beginning. Together, we can achieve anything."

As the sun rose, casting its golden light over the valley, Elara and Kael stood hand in hand, ready to face whatever the future held. Their hearts and souls were intertwined, their bond a beacon of light and love for all to see. And as they looked towards the horizon, they knew that their journey was far from over. Together, they were unstoppable, their love a force that transcended time and space.

Chapter 20: Eternal Desire

The sanctuary thrived, becoming a beacon of love and magic in Elysia. Under Elara and Kael's guidance, people from all corners of the realm came to learn, to heal, and to grow. The air was always filled with laughter, the rustling of pages from ancient tomes, and the gentle hum of magic. The sanctuary had become a testament to their love and the power of their bond.

One evening, as the sun dipped below the horizon and painted the sky in shades of orange and pink, Elara and Kael decided to take a walk through the gardens they had lovingly tended. The air was cool, the scent of blooming roses and jasmine wafting around them. Hand in hand, they strolled along the winding paths, their hearts full of contentment.

"Elara," Kael said softly, breaking the comfortable silence. "Do you ever think about what the future holds for us?"

Elara squeezed his hand, her eyes twinkling with affection. "Every day, Kael. I see us continuing to build this sanctuary, helping others find the strength in their bonds, just as we have. And most importantly, I see us growing old together, our love only deepening with time."

Kael smiled, pulling her closer. "I couldn't agree more. We've created something truly special here, but nothing compares to what we have between us."

As they reached a secluded part of the garden, Kael turned to face Elara, his expression serious yet filled with love. "There's something I've been wanting to do, Elara. Something that will symbolize our bond for all time."

Elara's heart fluttered as Kael reached into his pocket and pulled out a small, intricately carved wooden box. He opened it to reveal a ring, its band delicate yet strong, adorned with a brilliant gem that seemed to capture the light of the setting sun.

"Elara," Kael began, his voice trembling with emotion. "From the moment we met, I knew there was something extraordinary about you.

You have been my light, my strength, and my love. Will you marry me and make our bond eternal?"

Tears welled up in Elara's eyes as she looked at the ring, then at Kael. Her heart swelled with love and joy, and she nodded, her voice barely a whisper. "Yes, Kael. A thousand times yes."

Kael slipped the ring onto her finger, and they kissed, the world around them fading away as they sealed their commitment to each other. The magic of their love pulsed around them, a living testament to the strength of their bond.

As they pulled away, breathless and smiling, Kael took Elara's hand once more. "Let's make tonight a night to remember."

They walked back to their cabin, the anticipation and desire between them building with each step. The air was charged with magic and passion, a reflection of their deep connection.

Once inside, Kael lit a fire in the hearth, its warm glow casting dancing shadows on the walls. Elara watched him, her heart racing with love and desire. She moved to him, her fingers trailing lightly over his shoulders, her touch igniting a fire within him.

"Kael," she whispered, her voice trembling with emotion. "I want to celebrate our love, to feel every part of you."

Kael turned to her, his eyes dark with desire. "Elara, you are everything to me. Let's make this night unforgettable."

Their lips met in a passionate kiss, a fusion of love and longing that left them both breathless. Kael's hands roamed over her back, pulling her closer, deepening their connection. Elara could feel the heat between them, a fire that burned brighter with each touch, each caress.

"Kael," she moaned softly, her voice filled with need. "I need you."

Kael's eyes locked onto hers, his gaze filled with a mixture of love and desire. "And I need you, Elara. Always."

They moved together, their bodies pressing close, the heat between them almost unbearable. Kael's hands explored every curve and contour of her body, his touch leaving a trail of burning desire in its wake. Elara could feel the magic of their bond amplifying every sensation, every touch, creating a heady mix of pleasure and longing.

"Elara," Kael murmured against her skin, his voice filled with reverence and passion. "You drive me wild."

Elara's breath came in short gasps, her body trembling with the intensity of her feelings. "Kael," she whispered, her voice thick with desire. "I can't get enough of you."

Kael's lips claimed hers once more, the kiss deep and hungry, their bodies moving together in a dance of love and passion. Elara could feel the magic between them, a living, breathing force that amplified their every emotion. She felt as if they were merging into one, their bond a tangible force that pulsed with life.

As the night wore on, they explored the depths of their desire, their connection growing stronger with each passing moment. The fire crackled softly in the hearth, casting a warm glow over their entwined bodies. Elara felt a deep sense of peace and belonging, knowing that with Kael by her side, they could face anything.

"Kael," she whispered, her voice filled with emotion. "I love you."

Kael's hand cupped her cheek, his eyes shining with love. "And I love you, Elara. Forever."

As they lay together, wrapped in each other's arms, the world outside faded away, leaving only the warmth of their connection, the strength of their bond, and the depth of their love. And as they drifted off to sleep in each other's arms, Elara knew that whatever challenges lay ahead, they would face them together, their hearts and souls united by love and magic.

The sanctuary continued to thrive, a haven for those seeking to understand the magic of love and connection. Under Elara and Kael's guidance, bonds were forged, and lives were transformed. Their legacy grew, their names becoming synonymous with hope and love throughout Elysia.

As they stood together, watching the sunrise over their sanctuary, Elara felt a deep sense of fulfillment. They had created something beautiful, something lasting. And as long as they were together, their love would continue to inspire and guide others.

"Kael," she said softly, her voice filled with emotion. "This is just the beginning."

Kael smiled, his eyes filled with love. "Yes, Elara. Just the beginning. Together, we can achieve anything."

As the sun rose, casting its golden light over the valley, Elara and Kael stood hand in hand, ready to face whatever the future held. Their hearts and souls were intertwined, their bond a beacon of light and love for all to see. And as they looked towards the horizon, they knew that their journey was far from over. Together, they were unstoppable, their love a force that transcended time and space.